I0788103

How to read this book

Giraffe

This book has some hard words.

The first time you see a hard word

- the hard word is blue
- then you will see what the hard word means.

Bold

Not bold

Names are written in **bold.**

How to read this book

The pictures help you

understand the words.

You can ask for help to read

this story from

- a friend

- a family member

- or a support worker.

Hear us roar!

by **Casey Gray**

The hot sun burns

Stevie's face.

And melts **Kim's** protest sign.

A protest is when lots of people

get together to stand up for

what they want.

They have to walk all the way to town in the hot desert sun.

Because the taxi driver does not stop when he sees **Stevie** and **Kim**.

The taxi driver yells

I do not pick up disabled people!

The driver does not care that it is wrong.

As the taxi drives away

Stevie yells

You stupid **Grump**!

A **Grump** is a person who is

angry or rude.

Stevie and **Kim** get to

the protest.

Stevie is so hot from the walk.

She vomits on **Kim's** feet.

Kim is kind.

She does not get angry.

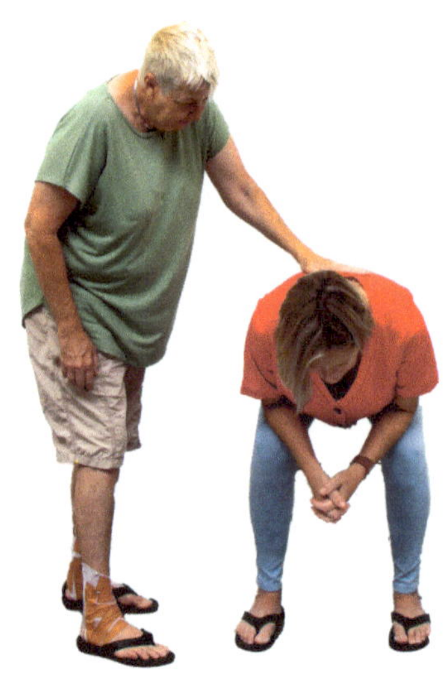

She pats **Stevie** on the back.

And says

My poor **Stevie-Wonder**.

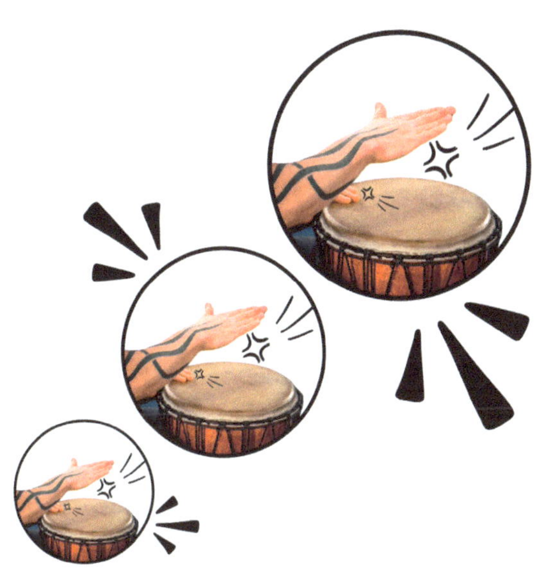

A drum beats

boom

boom-boom

boom.

The protesters yell

Hear us roar for Human

Rights Law!

Kim holds up her protest sign that says

Stop the **Grumps**!

Jax the dog and other protesters have disability pride flags.

Everyone roars.

But not the **Grumps**.

They yell mean words at

the protesters.

It makes the

protesters stronger.

The drum is as loud

as thunder.

Stevie's brain screams

Stop those **Grumps** before

someone gets hurt!

But people are too busy taking photos with their phones.

Stevie wants to help.

But she is frozen.

One **Grump** breaks **Kim's** protest sign.

The other **Grump** grabs **Kim** around the neck and drags her.

Stevie snaps out of being frozen.

She runs at the **Grumps**

Noooooooo!

One **Grump** asks **Stevie**

What are you going to do

about it short stuff?

Stevie rams the **Grump**.

And he falls onto the

other **Grump**.

Just like getting a strike at bowling.

A strike is when you get all the pins down.

Stevie is amazed she was so brave.

The protesters clap and roar.

Even **Jax** barks

I love you **Stevie**!

The police move in around the **Grumps**.

Handcuff those **Grumps**!

The **Grumps** will never drive a taxi again.

Kim yells

You are my super hero

Stevie-Wonder!

Stevie thinks about **Cow 569**.

Cow 569 was just a cow who

liked to eat grass with her bird.

Then **Cow 569** saved her farmer from a big flood.

Now people call her

Super Cow.

Stevie thinks

I am brave like **Super Cow**.

A nurse takes **Stevie** and **Kim**

to the ambulance.

The nurse says

Kim will be okay.

Stevie and **Kim** sit and watch a reporter.

A reporter is a person who tells the news.

He says

Today we saw people do bad things.

And we saw people do brave things.

The reporter asks

Do you want to say something **Stevie**?

Stevie says

Choose to be wonderful.

Say YES to getting a Human Rights Law.

It will help stop people being mean to people with disability.

Kim says

It will take a long time for everyone to be wonderful like you **Stevie-Wonder**.

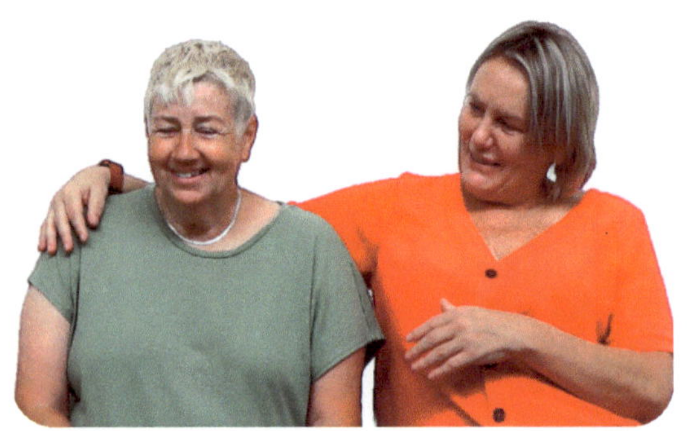

Stevie puts her arm around **Kim.**

Yes **Kim** but today we can rest.

The end.

A page to say thank you

Thank you **Sara** and **Randa** it was fun taking photos with you.

Thank you **Susan** and **Armando** and **crew** from the **Broken Hill Art Exchange** for giving me time to write and take photos inspired by community, red dust and blue sky.

Thank you to the people who tested this book to see if it is easy and fun to read.

Printing information

Hear us roar!

Author: **Casey Gray**

Published by **Books By ED**

Copyright © 2024 **Casey Gray, Books By ED**

Images copyright © 2024 **Casey Gray.** Stock images used under license.

ISBN: 978-0-6459693-0-6

Books By ED, Gosford NSW, Australia.

For more information https://www.byed.com.au/contact

Proudly supported by Creative Art Central, Central Coast Council, 2023.